by Ali Bovis   illustrated by Ada Abigael Aco

LEELA'S SWEET TREATS

International Night

biscotti

ladoo

Calico Kid

An Imprint of Magic Wagon
abdobooks.com

For Gabe and Becca, love you and our East End Avenue adventures always —AB

To Papa and Mama, who supported my career choices —AA

abdobooks.com

Published by Magic Wagon, a division of ABDO, PO Box 398166, Minneapolis, Minnesota 55439. Copyright © 2023 by Abdo Consulting Group, Inc. International copyrights reserved in all countries. No part of this book may be reproduced in any form without written permission from the publisher. Calico Kid™ is a trademark and logo of Magic Wagon.

Printed in the United States of America, North Mankato, Minnesota.
102022
012023

Written by Ali Bovis
Illustrated by Ada Abigael Aco
Edited by Bridget O'Brien
Art Directed by Candice Keimig

Library of Congress Control Number: 2022940058

Publisher's Cataloging-in-Publication Data

Names: Bovis, Ali, author. | Aco, Ada Abigael, illustrator.
Title: International night / by Ali Bovis ; illustrated by Ada Abigael Aco.
Description: Minneapolis, Minnesota : Magic Wagon, 2023. | Series: Leela's sweet treats
Summary: A big snowstorm threatens to wreck Leela and Liam's International Night at school, but they learn how to make the event the best it can be with limited supplies and resources.
Identifiers: ISBN 9781098235826 (lib. bdg.) | ISBN 9781098236526 (ebook) | ISBN 9781098236878 (Read-to-Me ebook)
Subjects: LCSH: Activity programs in education--Juvenile fiction. | Cultural awareness--Juvenile fiction. | Blizzards--Juvenile fiction. | Expectation (Psychology)--Juvenile fiction. | Adaptability (Psychology)--Juvenile fiction. | Best friends--Juvenile fiction.
Classification: DDC E--dc23

Table of Contents

Chapter 1

Snowy Day

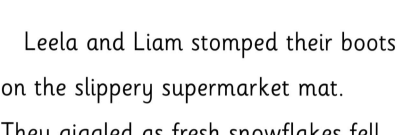

Leela and Liam stomped their boots on the slippery supermarket mat. They giggled as fresh snowflakes fell off their shoulders.

"Come on, kids," said Leela's mom, grabbing the last shopping cart. "We'd better hurry. It's snowing outside, but it looks like a tornado in here."

Leela looked around. Mom was right. The supermarket was a mess, and it was busier than the subway station at rush hour!

There were people everywhere. People with bread. People with water. People with meat, mini-marshmallows, cream of mushroom soup, and more.

"Whoops," said Liam, tripping over an empty crate.

"Yikes," said Leela, bumping into a baby carriage.

"Careful," said Mom. "Everyone must be stocking up for the storm. Let's see your list so we can get ready for the big night."

A smile bloomed in the corners of Leela's cold cheeks. International Night at school was going to be big, all right!

Leela yanked out some sticky notes. "I've got a bunch of things ready at home. But I still need ingredients for this one— the yummiest of all!"

Leela balanced on her tippy toes and grabbed grated coconut off a shelf. She crouched and plucked baking chocolate from a box.

"We'll have the sweetest International Night in the history of Taylor Elementary," she whispered.

"Leela," yelled Liam from the refrigerated aisle. "Come quick! There's no milk!"

Chapter 2
Two Ladoos

"Howdy!" said Al, shoveling snow off the sidewalk as Leela, Liam, and Mom sloshed into the building.

Leela hurried to the elevator as
Mom got the mail.

Leela thought of everything she had already baked. Her naan to celebrate Dad's family from India was ready. Her biscotti to celebrate Mom's family from Italy was ready too.

But her ladoo was not, and she couldn't make it without milk. "Mom, Liam, please hurry," she called. International Night was in just two hours. There was no time to waste!

When they got home, Leela peeled
off her coat and boots. She waved to
Dad and dashed to the kitchen.

"Hi Ladoo!" she cheered to her bunny nibbling carrots in her crate. She started to haul out cooking supplies. "You won't be the only ladoo in the kitchen today!"

Hopefully . . .

A second later, Leela heard a knock. "Make way for the milk," cheered Liam, clutching the carton like a trophy.

"Phew!" Leela had never seen the supermarket out of milk. Thank goodness Liam had some at home to share. Leela poured the milk into a pot with the grated coconut and stirred.

Soon Leela rolled the mixture into balls and turned to Liam. "It's great the supermarket had the recyclable plates and compostable cups you wanted."

"Yep," Liam agreed, dipping a spoon in for a taste. "Especially since so much other stuff was missing."

Leela's eyebrows lifted as she pulled out the chocolate. Liam had a point. "Hopefully everyone else found what they needed too!"

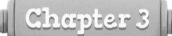

Chapter 3
The Big Night

Trill! Trill! Trill!

Two-thirds of a steel drum band greeted Leela, Liam, and Rebecca at school.

"Welcome to International Night!" said Principal Henderson. She handed out passport booklets. "You'll get a stamp from every country's table."

19

"Thanks," said Rebecca, taking a passport. She pulled the foil off her platter and turned to Leela and Liam. "Don't forget to visit me at the Israel table!"

Leela and Liam nodded.

Liam pointed to the drummers. "Cool!"

"Principal Henderson, where is the other one?" asked Leela, noticing three drums but only two drummers.

"It's taking her longer to get across town because of the storm," Principal Henderson answered. "Some other folks are running late too."

Leela spied the snow falling on West End Avenue through a window. Yikes! Hopefully everyone would make it.

kebab   manti

Leela and Liam tossed their jackets on a pile in the corner.

Scents of scones, samosas, taquitos, and kebabs swirled in Leela's nose. Her mouth watered.

Leela set out her platters as Liam went to pass out the cups and plates.

biscotti

ladoo

naan

23

Flags, maps, artifacts, and photos from all different countries crammed the cafeteria.

But as Leela looked closer,
she saw that at many tables
something was very wrong!

biscotti

ladoo

naan

Chapter 4

Come Together

Leela needed to find Liam.

She passed Manuel at the Mexico table shaking maracas. But something was missing.

She passed Kumiko at the Japan table demonstrating karate. But something was missing.

She passed Sofia at the Switzerland table mixing fondue. But something was missing.

Finally, Leela found Liam at the United States table.

"Hi!" he cheered through a mouth full of popcorn.

Leela pointed to a chocolate-chip cookies sign. "Look!" she said. "There are no cookies!"

"I heard it was because of the storm," Liam replied.

"That's not all," said Leela. "There are no chips in Mexico, no noodles in Japan, and no bread in Switzerland. The stores must have been sold out."

"Oh no!" said Liam.

"It's terrible!" said Leela, slumping her shoulders. "I wish I could help them like you helped me. But how?"

An announcement came over the speakers. "Get ready to come together for the Parade of Nations!"

chocolate chip cookies

Come together? An idea burst into Leela's head.

Leela wouldn't have been able to make her ladoo without Liam's milk. Friends share. Maybe countries could share too!

Leela grabbed Liam and huddled with their friends.

The countries came together.

Greece shared with Mexico.

China shared with Japan.

France shared with Switzerland.

And when the third drummer called to say she was going to be even later, Principal Henderson showed off her drumming skills!

After the Parade of Nations, the learning and tasting tours came to a close. There was just one thing left to do . . .